Contents

Leeches

Brandon Robshaw

Published in association with
The Basic Skills Agency

Hodder & Stoughton

A MEMBER OF THE HODDER HEADLINE GROUP

Acknowledgements
Cover: Barry Downard
Illustrations: Chris Coady

Orders: please contact Bookpoint Ltd, 130 Milton Park, Abingdon, Oxon OX14 4SB. Telephone: (44) 01235 827720, Fax: (44) 01235 400454. Lines are open from 9.00–6.00, Monday to Saturday, with a 24 hour message answering service. You can also order through our website: www.hodderheadline.co.uk.

British Library Cataloguing in Publication Data
A catalogue record for this title is available from The British Library

ISBN 0 340 87666 2

First published 2003
This edition published 2002
Impression number 10 9 8 7 6 5 4 3 2 1
Year   2007 2006 2005 2004 2003

Copyright © Brandon Robshaw 2003

Typeset by SX Composing DTP, Rayleigh, Essex.
Printed in Great Britain for Hodder & Stoughton Educational, a division of Hodder Headline, 338 Euston Road, London NW1 3BH by Athenaeum Press, Gateshead, Tyne and Wear.

1

The Leech Tank

The shed was dim.
No sun got in.
There were blinds at the windows.
The lights were low.

In the centre of the shed
stood a large glass tank.
There was a cover on top.

The tank was full of water.
The water was full of leeches.
Hundreds of them.
Small, black creatures.

Like worms, but flat.
Some were swimming.
Others stuck to the glass sides
of the tank.

Tim watched them.
He sat in a chair
with a cup of tea in his hand.
He had a plate of biscuits
on his lap.
Chocolate biscuits.
He liked watching his leeches.
He found it restful.

Drip. Drip. Drip.
What was that?
Tim put his biscuits down.
Drip. Drip. Drip.

Water was dripping from somewhere.
Tim frowned.
He got up.
He walked over to the tank.
Then he saw it.

One of the pipes that led to the tank
was leaking.
Drip. Drip. Drip.
There was already a big puddle
on the tiled floor.

Tim ran out of the shed.
He ran into his house.
He had to get a plumber –
and quickly!

2
The Plumber

Tim found the Yellow Pages.
He flipped through the book quickly.
There it was – 'Plumbers'.
About twenty pages of plumbers.
It shouldn't be too hard to get one.

It was harder than he thought.
The first plumber he called
was out on a job.
So was the second one.
The third said he could come round
in three days.
'That will be too late!' said Tim.

He called another plumber.
This time he got an answering machine.
He didn't bother to leave a message.

He was starting to get worried.
If that leak wasn't fixed soon,
it would get worse.
All the water might spill out.
Then all his leeches would die.

He ran his finger down the page.
'Martin Dudley, Master Plumber.'
Martin Dudley?
He knew that name.
Martin Dudley.
Oh yes, he knew that name all right.

A chill of fear went through him
at the memory.

3
The Bully

Tim remembered his schooldays
Martin Dudley had made his life a misery,
every day for years.
He was a big kid with a nasty streak.
A bully.
He bullied lots of kids,
but Tim most of all.

Every break,
Martin Dudley made him
turn out his pockets.
If there was any money there,
Martin Dudley took it.

He used to punch Tim.
Kick him.
Spit on him.
Knock him over and sit on him.

Once, he picked him up
and dropped him head first
into a bin.
Anther time, he pushed Tim's head
down the toilet and pulled the chain.
Tim thought he was going to drown.

It wasn't just the violence.
In a way, the insults were worse.
'You're a loser,'
Dudley would say to him.
'You're such a sad case.
What are you ever going to do in life?
Why don't you just die now, loser?'

For years,
Tim dreaded going to school.

That was a long time ago now.
Twenty-five years ago.
Seeing the name on the page
brought it all back.
It was like yesterday.
Tim realised he was trembling
with fear and anger.

He pulled himself together.
This might not even be
the same Martin Dudley.
It was quite a common name.

Even if it was the same one,
Dudley would be an adult now.
If he ever remembered
what he did at school,
he probably felt sorry about it.
If he met Tim now,
he might even say sorry.
That would make Tim feel
a lot better.

Anyway, he shouldn't be thinking of himself.
He had to save his leeches.
He quickly dialled Dudley's number.

'Martin Dudley here.'
Tim couldn't tell if it was
the same Martin Dudley or not.
A person's voice changes a lot
in twenty-five years.

'I've got a problem,' said Tim.
'A leaking pipe.
It's an emergency.'

'OK,' said the voice.
'I'll be right over.'

Tim gave him the address.
Half an hour later,
Dudley pulled up outside.

4
Making a Living

Tim knew him as soon as
he got out of the car.
He'd changed a lot, of course.
He'd got a lot fatter, and gone bald.
He still had the same chunky build.
He had the same annoying grin.
He walked with the same strut.

'What's the problem then, mate?'
asked Dudley.
Tim realised that Dudley
didn't recognise him.
That was a good thing.

'My leech tank's got a leak.'

'Leech tank?
What's that then, mate?'

'I'll show you.'

Tim took Dudley to the shed.
'There, you see?
Here it is.
And there's the leak.'

Dudley stared at the tank.
'What are those black things
swimming about in it?'

'Leeches.
They're like worms that live
in the water.
They suck blood.'

Dudley looked at him strangely.

'Very nice,' he said.
'What do you want
to keep things like that for?
Pets, are they?'

'No, they're not pets.
I breed them to sell.
They are used in hospitals.
They help to heal wounds, you see.
They suck away the blood
and prevent swellings.
I sell them to hospitals
all over the country.
It's how I make my living.'

Dudley laughed.
'We've all got to make a living,
I suppose.
It wouldn't suit me, though!
'Orrible things!'

5

'Should I tell him who I am?'

Dudley opened his bag of tools.
'Shouldn't take long to fix this.'

Tim watched him.
A question kept going through his mind.
Should I tell him who I am?

What would Dudley say if he knew?
He'd get a shock.
Surely he'd feel a bit ashamed of himself.

It would be a small way for Tim
to get his own back.

Maybe Dudley would say sorry.
That would make Tim feel better.

Dudley was kneeling on the floor,
taking his tools out.
Tim coughed.
'Er, you don't know who I am, do you?'

6

Laughter

Dudley looked round at him.
'No, should I?'

I'm Tim Robbins.'

Dudley stared at him.
'Tim . . . ?'
Slowly, understanding came into his eyes.
He pointed at Tim.
'Little Timmy Robbins!
Well, I'll be—'
He burst out laughing.

It was a long, loud laugh.
Not a nice laugh at all.
A mocking laugh.

Tim felt his face going red.
'Why are you laughing?'

'I can't help it!' said Dudley.
'To think of you – I mean,
you were such a little loser at school!
And then you end up keeping
these slimy little animals!
I mean, it's just the sort of thing
you *would* do, you loser!'

He turned back to his toolbag,
still laughing.
He got busy on the pipe.
Every now and then,
another laugh burst out.

Tim stood behind him, watching.
Dudley's bald head
was about an arm's length away from him.
He felt like swinging his fist and —

He pulled himself together.
'Would you like a cup of tea?' he asked.

'Yes, Timmy, you do that for me.
A nice cup of tea
and a few biscuits, mate.
That would hit the spot!'

Tim went back into the house
to make the tea.
Inside, he was boiling with rage.

7
Something Terrible

'Here's the tea,' said Tim.
'And chocolate biscuits too.'

The dripping had stopped.
Dudley was crouched down
checking his work.
His tools were spread around him.

Tim put the tray down on the floor.
It was just near a large, iron spanner.

Dudley didn't look round.
He reached behind him for a biscuit.

'The pipe should be OK now,' he said.
'Your little pets will be fine.'
He laughed again.
'Little Timmy Robbins,
the leech keeper!
Just the sort of thing
a loser like you would do!'

Tim stared at the top
of Dudley's bald head.
The rage inside him
began to boil over.
He knew he was going to do
something terrible.
He couldn't stop himself.

He didn't *want* to stop himself.

He took a quiet step forward.
He picked up the iron spanner.
He raised it above Dudley's bald head.

8

'Where am I?'

'Where am I? said Dudley.
His head was aching.
He had no idea where he was.
He was sitting in a tank of water
in a dim room.
The water came up to his chin.
A man was sitting in a chair, watching him.
'Who are you?' asked Dudley.

'Don't you remember?
I'm Tim Robbins. You know?
The kid you used to bully at school.
The loser. The leech keeper.'

It all slowly came back to Dudley.
Little Timmy Robbins.
Yes, he'd fixed his leech tank.
He'd had a bit of a laugh about it.
And then . . .
he couldn't remember the next bit.

'What happened?' he asked.

'I gave you a tap on the head,'
said Tim.
'With a spanner.
And now you're in the leech tank.
That's a bit of a surprise for you,
isn't it?'

Dudley stared at him for a minute.
Was this all some horrible dream?
No, it wasn't a dream.
The cold water was all too real.
'I'll kill you for this, Robbins!' he swore.
He tried to jump out of the tank.

He couldn't get up.
His hands and feet were tied together.
He looked down and saw the rope.

He saw something else, too.
He had been stripped naked.
All over his body
were little slimy black creatures.
On his arms and legs,
on his chest, on his belly.

'This is a joke, isn't it?' he said hoarsely.
'Tell me it's a joke!'

'It's no joke,' said Tim.
'You're helping me feed my leeches.
You won't feel any pain.
They have a kind of anaesthetic
in their saliva.
Wonderful creatures.'

'They – they're sucking my blood!'

'That's right,' said Tim.
'Bless them.'

'But I'll die!
I'll die from loss of blood!'

'That's right,' said Tim.
'It'll take a good few hours, though.'

Dudley began to scream.
Tim took a drink of tea.
He nibbled a chocolate biscuit.
He enjoyed watching Dudley
feeding his leeches.

He found it restful.